Five Little Bunnies Hopping on a Hill

To Rachel and Gina
–S.M.

To Elizabeth and Stephen
–L.J.B.

ISBN 0-439-80382-9

12 11 10 9 8 7 6 5 4   6 7 8 9 10 11/0

Printed in the U.S.A.   40
First printing, March 2006

Five Little Bunnies Hopping on a Hill

by Steve Metzger
Illustrated by
Laura J. Bryant

SCHOLASTIC INC.
New York Toronto London Auckland Sydney
Mexico City New Delhi Hong Kong Buenos Aires

Five little bunnies hopping on a hill.

One bunny tripped and took a spill.

The mother called the doctor and the doctor said,

"No more bunnies hopping on a hill!"

Four little bunnies digging messy holes.

One bunny found a sleeping mole!

The mother called the doctor and the doctor said,

"No more bunnies digging messy holes!"

Three little bunnies playing by the sea.

One got scared by a buzzing bee.

The mother called the doctor and the doctor said,

"No more bunnies playing by the sea!"

Two little bunnies dancing in the park.

One got lost when it grew dark.

The mother called the doctor and the doctor said,

"No more bunnies dancing in the park!"

One little bunny spinning 'round and 'round.

Got so dizzy she fell to the ground.

The mother called the doctor and the doctor said,

"No more bunnies spinning 'round and 'round!"

Now there are . . .
No little bunnies playing in the sun.
No little bunnies having any fun.

The mother called the doctor and the doctor said,

"Let those bunnies run, run, RUN!"